What this book is about

Ordsall Writers published their first collection of writing in 2011, a book full of stories, poems and songs from all members of the group, first heard at their weekly Creative Writing sessions. In 2013, thanks to a grant from the Heritage Lottery Fund, the group had the opportunity to put together a new collection – this time with the theme of 'History and Heritage'.

The project was part of the BBC's initiative, 'All Our Stories', which included oral history and recordings of people's memories, some of which were broadcast on radio in 2012 and 2013. Luckily, the Ordsall group had a rich archive of material to draw on for inspiration, provided by Salford LIDS, a collection of interviews and conversations dating back over many years, and mainly featuring older people from East Salford. That's why the Ordsall project was called 'East Salford's Heritage Heard', as the members felt it gave the chance for these voices to reach a wider audience at last.

Thanks to Mike and Jane of Salford LIDS for making this material available, and a special thanks to all the people who contributed their stories and memories to the audio archive over the years. This collection is now available on the internet, thanks to the funding from Heritage Lottery, and this book was simply inspired by the strange and wonderful things we have listened to, over the last few months.

Cover photos: c. Zodiac Films

An 'Ordsall Writers' collection: Book 2

Part of 'All Our Stories' project, BBC 2013

by

Residents of Ordsall, Salford

"The Wednesday group"

FOREWORD

by

Steve Pilling

A paperback book from Lulu.com
This is the Millenium Edition 2013

A CIP catalogue record is available for this edition from the British Library.

An ISBN has been issued for this version
ISBN: 978-1-291-59343-3

Layout, typesetting of a sort and presentation of this edition has been organised by Mike Scantlebury and delivered by Lulu.com

Printed at the behest of Lulu.com who can be found at http://www.Lulu.com/

CONTENTS

DEDICATION

Ordsall Writers is an Ordsall Trust project. The Creative group meets on a Wednesday morning from 10 to 12 noon at Ordsall Community Arts in Salford and works on a variety of projects, producing songs, stories and poems on a regular basis. Thanks to funding from the Heritage Lottery Fund, we have been able to focus this year on listening to stories from older people in the area, their memories and history, and it has been an exciting and vital inspiration to us all.

Foreword by Steve Pilling

'The man who sank the Bismark'

My name is Steve Pilling and I own The Damson restaurant on Salford Quays.

Recently, on a summer's day in 2013, a small group of local writers came to my place for lunch and I was happy to tell them my story. They said they might put it into a book. They were so confident, I said that if they ever brought the book out, I would help them launch it at my restaurant.

Let's see if that ever comes true!

My Story:

My father, Thomas Pilling, joined the navy in World War Two at the age of 16 years (although he should have been 18 before he did so). He served on a ship called HMS Devonshire. One day, word came through that The Bismark had just sunk a ship called The Robin Hood. HMS Devonshire retaliated and sank The Bismark with a torpedo. The crew were later reprimanded for this, as they hadn't received their proper orders before they took action.

Still, when my father was in hospital, many years later, I put a notice over his hospital bed which read: 'Tommy (Thomas) Pilling, the man who sank The Bismark'.

After the war my Dad worked for the Gas and Electricity Boards. He told me there was an unwritten code amongst the workers that if they were sent to cut the gas or electricity off to a single woman with children, they would go round later and re-connect it. They were only too aware that there a lot of young war widows in those days. He said that one workman did cut off the supply to a single mother, but then did nothing about re-connecting her. My dad was so incensed, he went straight along to the local pub and sorted the guy out who had failed to do what he should.

Members of the writer's group asked me why the restaurant is called 'The Damson'. My reply is that my mother worked for Christies who made cotton goods, i.e. towels, bedding etc. Most of the girls, including my mother, were called 'The Damson Girls' as their arms were that colour after working with the damson skins which were used to dye the cotton goods.

Story written by Sylvia Sharples, as narrated by Steve Pilling.

August 2013

Recently, Ordsall Creative Writing Group went for a celebratory meal at the Damson Restaurant on Salford Quays, at the end of a grant-funded Heritage project. The proprietor asked us if we had enjoyed our meal, which we told him was excellent. He asked us about our group and when we told him about the work we had been doing collecting heritage, memories and tales from the past, he was only too happy to share his own stories. Thanks, Steve.

Sylvia Sharples

Isaac Street

We were living in Salford 7 when I was expecting my second child. Because of being burgled I could never settle and decided to look for another property to live in. I remember going to Manchester with my mum and putting a deposit down on a two bedroom property, 34 Isaac Street, which was owned by a private landlord. My Husband Fred, our son Carl, daughter Janet and I lived in Isaac Street Salford 5 from 1971 till roughly about 1974/5.

The house we lived in had no bathroom, just two bedrooms, a living room, a kitchen with a belson sink with a lean-to, plus a cellar, and the toilet was outside in the back yard. In those days we had a coal fire and the coal used to be delivered down the coal chute straight into the cellar. In the cellar an old fashioned mangle was bolted to the floor although I never used it. The cellar did not have an electric light and could be very eerie if you had to go down for coal in the evening. Nearly everyone who lived in Isaac Street would own a tin bath to bathe in.

If you did not have your chimney swept on a regular basis the coal fire when lit would blow out and fill up the living room with a cloud of smoke from the chimney, which used to happen a few times when we first moved there (this seemed to happen especially if we had visitors). The soot when swept would be put in bags and stored in the lean-to till it could be moved.

I took a ginger tom cat in off the streets because I felt sorry for it as it was crying and hungry - little did I know that it was a wild tom cat which could not be tamed.

It would pinch raw frozen chicken off the table and jump on the bags of soot tear them open leaving soot everywhere. Oh, what a mess I would have to clean up.

The living room window was coloured leaded glass and I remember us looking after my sister-in-law's dog which was called Blackie while she went on holiday. I came back from shopping to find the window broken and that Blackie had escaped, having decided to jump through the window to try and get back to where he lived which was in Clayton, Manchester. (How he managed that, to this day we don't know).

In those days people would burn a lot of their rubbish on the coal fire during the day and I remember one night we were in bed asleep and the fires were out as we thought. Around about 2.00am in the morning we were woken up with smoke coming out of the chimney in the bedroom. Fire engines arrived because of smoke coming from the bedroom chimney and the kitchen was full of smoke as the electrics in the kitchen had set on fire. Apparently paper which had been burnt through the day was stuck and smouldering in the chimney. The whole street was woken up and outside in their nightwear- all the neighbours supported us with blankets and cups of tea.

St Clements Church was being run by a young male vicar who used to wear a long black cloak. Unfortunately, I cannot remember his name. He was very popular in the area and had a regular congregation of young women who would all fancy him.

Although we only lived for a short time in Isaac Street, it was one of the best and happiest places we lived in. I remember being able to leave your front door open and never having to worry about anyone trying to burgle you and you could stand out on the front step at any time of the day or night.

Your neighbours, whether at the top or bottom of the street would always find the time to talk to you, everyone looked out for each other. You could go for a night out, come back in the early hours of the morning and would be able to walk down the old Trafford Road on your own and be safe.

Berry Kent, September 2013

If God Created Salford

If God created Salford,
We wouldn't have the Height,
And Brindle Heath and Hanky Park
just wouldn't feel that right
I don’t think there'd be Pendleton,
Ordsall, Duchy, Weaste
lslington and Langworthy
would suddenly just cease
Broughton would be rolling hills,
And Kersal fields of green.
Swinton still a pig farm,
And Worsley it would seem
To be a church set on its own,
With fields for miles around,
And Eccles would be far too small,
To be thought of as a town
But Salford's not made,
by an immortal in the sky,
It’s made from sweat and blood of man,
And pain that made us cry
These dirty streets contain our love,
our past, our dreams, our fears
lt’s not just bricks and mortar,
But the struggle through the years
But for all the change it's still the same,
I know it may seem odd
This city came from man,
Much more than just from God.

Chris Thorn

My name is Madge Bown. I was born in Ordsall in the City of Salford. I have been a member of the Writers' Group since 2010.

In the last twelve months since our last book, I have written a number of poems, songs and stories. I have found the group to be very friendly and helpful. I look forward to Wednesday mornings, the sessions are very interesting as each member has different talents. I hope we can continue to enjoy our creative writing.

The Wedding Day

The bride and groom stepped out of the church and the groom asked if anyone would take some photographs. A friend dashed forward saying, 'I will do it'.

It was the beginning of August and the day was dull and overcast, but the couple were hoping for a break in the clouds, so that he could take some good photographs for their album. They both stood waiting for him to say, 'Are you ready?' but the words never came: he had taken the picture and was now taking some more outside the church. When the photographs were developed the groom looked as if he was waiting for something to happen and the bride waiting to be told to smile. The other photos only had men on them, not a wife or girl friend in sight.

Everyone arrived at the tripe shop on Eccles New Road for a meal and the camera came out again. A two-tier wedding cake stood at the end of the table in front of the bride and groom, and yes, he did it again, the photo showed the wedding cake and the groom peeping round it, but the bride was missing.

After the meal everyone went to the local pub where for some unknown reason the bride decided to sing a song. She could not remember all the words and the pianist was not too sure how the tune went, but they did get a clap and the bride got a big smile from the groom.

A little later in the evening one of the guests was sick. He lived a bus ride away so the groom took him to his home and lent him a shirt and a suit. When they returned there was a lot of good humoured laughter as the groom was five foot eight and the guest was over six foot and had long legs. The jacket could have done with two or three inches on the sleeves and the trousers to say the least, were quite short.

A relative invited them all back to her place where sandwiches had been laid on for everyone. Some of the older people decided to go home as it was getting late. The relative lived over a shop on Trafford Road. You entered through the back door, then up a set of stairs into an odd shaped sitting room. The shop was on a corner hence the odd shape. They ate the sandwiches danced and played games. In one of the games everyone had to roll their dress, skirt or trousers up over their knees then a man or woman had to guess who they were. A woman went first but lost because she did not recognise her husband's legs. A man was next. He went round the circle and guessed a lady's name, giving him another try. He again guessed the same lady's name, who happened to be the bride. The groom was not happy and he stopped the game, much to everybody's relief as the man's wife, a large red-headed woman, looked ready to hit him.

The bride and groom made their way to the groom's home where they were going to stay until they got a house of their own. He knocked on the door but could not get an answer so they walked round the back and into the yard. He picked up pieces of coal out of the bunker and threw them at the window of his mother's bedroom but she did not appear.

“What are we going to do now?” asked his new wife. “Hold my coat for a minute,” he asked her. “I will climb on the wall.” He climbed up the back door and onto the wall. He was a little unsteady as he made his way towards the window.

Placing his hand on the house wall for support, he leaned over and banged on the bedroom window. After a few minutes his mother opened the curtains and peeped out. “Open the door,” her son shouted as she rubbed her eyes, unable to believe her son was balanced on a six inch-wide wall at nearly two o'clock in the morning.

A short time later the door opened and they entered the house, they both sat down and gave a sigh of relief. It was a wedding day to remember but maybe not for the right reasons.

Madge Bown (The Bride)

Irony in Death

A few years ago my mother and I were both widowed in the same year.

When arranging my husband's funeral, it was complicated as he had a grown-up family who were about my age. I was staying with friends in Wales, and the funeral was arranged, believe it or not for Red Nose Day. My friend asked if I wanted a red rose to put in the grave - (red rose for Red Nose day). The irony was unbelievable, and it just broke the ice. He was taken in a Rolls Royce hearse, the best transport available.

On arrival for the graveside ceremony, at the foot of the grave were his children and ex-wife, the men wearing long dark overcoats, all spread out in a line, it looked like a scene from The Godfather. My father positioned himself with his back to a tree as if he thought something might happen. It didn't - but we all made a swift exit when the ceremony was over.

A few months later my father passed away. On the way to the crematorium we were led by a refuse wagon with the word "Vulture" on the back. Mother saw the funny side of this. After his funeral, a couple came up and thanked my mother for a lovely service, they had really enjoyed it - but they thought it was another person's funeral with the same name!

I was living with my mother - as we had both been recently widowed - the mix-ups with phone calls regarding inscriptions on graves and memorials were very hard to believe. Truth is stranger than fiction! At times it was like a theatre farce. You had to have a sense of humour to get through that dark period. The old adage, laughter is only a hair's breadth from crying was very true on these occasions.

Sylvia Sharples
May 2011

Back Yard Bookie

Before I start my tale the one thing you should know is that betting hasn't always been legal and in the 1950's it was most definitely illegal. Today you can walk down any high street and find a betting shop but in the 1950's the placing of a bet was a cloak and dagger affair.

Now Mrs H was a woman of her time. She worked long hours in the local cotton mill to pay her bills and put food on the table. What little there was left over at the end of the week was hers to spend as she pleased. In Mrs H's case this was the forbidden pleasure of a flutter on the horses.

Now this being illegal the only way to place a bet was with a back yard bookie. Most houses were back to back terraces, each with a small yard which backed on to an alleyway between terraces. It was in these yards that the business of placing a bet took place.

Each area had its own bookie and Mrs H was a regular customer to her local back yard bookie. Each week she would place a small wager on the outcome of a horse race. A shilling each way was her regular bet but on this occasion that bet didn't pay off. Why you ask? Not because her horse fell or came in last. No, Mrs H's downfall came via the long arm of the law. For one the one thing Mrs H couldn't do was run! So when the police came a calling Mrs H was just too slow!

As was the practice if the police showed up, everyone would do a runner - but being middle aged and having to work long hours, running was not something our Mrs H was good at. Being the only one the police could catch Mrs H had to take the fall.

Mrs H was brought before the bench to answer for her crime and having been caught in the act she had no option but to plead guilty and the judge duly passed sentence.

But don't despair - for whilst betting was a criminal offence the penalty wasn't hard labour or six months in jail but simply a fine. But could a poor working class woman pay the fine? Where would she get the money from? Well, these bookies took care of their own, and whilst Mrs H took the fall she didn't pay the fine. No - that was all part of doing business and the bookie made sure Mrs H wasn't out of pocket.

You would think that Mrs H had learnt her lesson and would never place a bet again. No the very next week she was back laying down her bet with the very same back yard bookie!

Elaine Sutcliffe
September 2013

Backstreet Bookies

As a kid in Salford the things I saw
Like people queuing at a back-entry door
People moving in a suspicious way
Up to no good some would say

A man dogging out at each back-entry end
This lucrative trade they must defend
Well, people liked to have a bet
But it wasn't legal yet

Son go and place my bet
If you move yourself you won't get wet
A bit of rain never hurt a fly
If I win think what we'll buy

Later that day the news was good
What will I get, dad said he would?
Down the entry I went once more
To the slide back window in the back door
I gave the code that only we know

Busty and DVP 85
Out came the money and snakes alive
They both had done really good
What will I get, well - they said I would

Thanks son, now go out and play
You cheeky bugger, what did you say

You get a clip, that'll be your lot
You should be thankful for what you’ve got

Then later that day my name rang out
Get in now or you’ll get a clout
Take my bet and put it on
It must be you “you're lucky, son”

Once more down the entry I did go
What I said under my breath, only I know
Well, I did hope my luck ran out
Why be lucky if they give you nowt?

Ken Phoenix

(Ordsall born, now living in Australia)

That's why I love Swinton

If you travel down the East Lancs Road,
You'll find the place I'm from
You won't find any palaces
Cathedrals there are none
My street is Moorside Road,
There's not a moor in sight
The stations at the top,
On the left, not on the right,
The precinct's where we shop
Alas, the shops have all closed down,
But nobody here is worried
There's a rumour going round,
Asda's on the way
So salvation is quite near
But it won't be like our precinct,
And that's what people fear
There's lot's of pubs at night,
And if you want to dine,
There's food from every nation,
And the quality is fine
So that's why I love Swinton
I know it's not the best,
But my heart's in Swinton,
And it's better than the rest.

Chris Thorn

Aunty Vera

Aunty Vera lived at number 1 Regent Square. She said they moved there from further down the road because the corner house was an inch longer than the other houses on the square but they had to pay a little bit more because of it. When I first met her in about 2004 she lived with her brother Tommy Brennan at No. 2 Regent Square. Tommy was active on the committees in the New Barracks and I loved him because at any meeting Tommy was in he would get up and leave if it went on after a certain time, which usually meant that the meeting would then finish.

I went round to record Aunty Vera in her house in the early days of the recording project. Leslie Holmes, our next door neighbour and Lads Club activist told me that she was renowned for her stories and had lived on Regent Square all her life. I had never met her before as she was mostly housebound. I never asked her age but she looked in her 70's and was very smiley and welcoming I saw her out of the house only once when she was pushed down to the Lowry to see her grand niece dance. She sat in a large chair in the living room with everything she needed around her easily accessible. She had a newspaper with the racing form face up and put a daily bet on, which was picked up by Derek who called in every day and was a great friend. Our first recording was inaudible as I had pressed the wrong button, so I had to return and some stories told here may be from my memory.

I was amazed when she told me her father's job was a cattle drover as our area was rows and rows of terraced houses and

Regent Road in those days. Apparently, there was a cattle market on Cross St. and her father's job was to herd the cattle through the back streets down to the 'abataire'. Every time I heard the abattoire mentioned it was always pronounced like this. Aunty Vera's father did this job until he was 72 and loved it. I heard lots of stories over the years about the journey the cows made through the narrow back streets of Ordsall. Apparently it was a noisy business and when the cattle and sometimes sheep were heard approaching everyone rushed to close the doors as it was not unknown to find a cow in the hall. One woman told me she always felt sorry for the animals being driven to their deaths. She said they always looked so scared. People told me that that having the abbatoire close by was a blessing in those days when hunger was common because they could usually get bones to be boiled up for a stew if the dockers had not been picked for work that day. Derek told me stories about as youngsters the children would go out to the country in the cattle trucks and help to round up the animals and they had to be very careful to avoid their backsides or they would be in trouble with their mothers when they got home for "stinking the place out". Derek said he enjoyed those days out and they got a few pennies for their work.

The phrases I heard repeatedly were 'times were hard in them days', 'we were all in the same boat' and 'we didn't know any different'. The pawn shop was well used and Aunty Vera told of how when she passed the shop once she noticed there was a dress just the same as she had worn at the Whit Walks. She told a story of how her mother's friend was paid the day before the rent was due and how she lent it to them and that was repaid the day Vera's dad got his wages.

Christmas was very different from today and 'Wood St. Mission' provided a party with a pork pie and an orange. I heard from one lady how she caught diphtheria at one of those parties. Not a very great gift. Diphtheria was quite common in those days and I have a vivid memory of one very old man remembering with tears in his eyes how he called back from the Army and was holding hands with his 12 year old brother when he died. His father had visited the isolation hospital where his brother was and seen through the window the child in the next bed drinking from the flower bowl because he was so thirsty. His dad had gone in to the Ward, picked him up and carried him for the few miles back home." No son of his was going to die of thirst".

Auntie Vera died a couple of years ago now. She eventually moved down the road to sheltered accommodation in latter years, and was in and out of hospital. Her wonderful niece Bev, (my over the road neighbour), cared for her for many years and described her as a second mum. That's the way people are in Ordsall.

Thanks to all for your wonderful stories.

Jane Wood

False Alarm

I was born in Manchester just before the war in 1937. My father worked at Gorton Railway Depot as a welder.

In 1941 my father was transferred to Bow Railway Depot in London. He had been unable to enlist in the armed forces, despite trying under different names. Welding was a designated trade and as such these tradesmen were not allowed to enlist as they were needed to keep all the services going throughout the country.

Our new home was in Romford, Essex which in those days was a small rural town outside of London. At the time there were many air raids and the use of cluster bombs was normal. These bombs were on a timer and all you could hear was a loud ticking before the delayed explosion.

On one occasion there was an air raid and something hit the roof of the house and then there was silence and my mother woke me, picked up my baby brother and we were all rushing to get to the shelter. As we came onto the upstairs landing my mother said to my father "Go into the loft and see if it's landed as I can hear it ticking".

My father, naturally obeyed, and went into the loft but couldn’t find anything. My mother urged him to look in the adjoining loft, there being a gap he could get through. He shouted that he couldn’t find anything.

He came back to the loft opening and before my mother could speak, my father said "You silly ***, no wonder you can hear ticking you've got the alarm clock under your arm!"

So the panic was over and we made our way to the shelter where we stayed until the raid was over.

My father never let my mother forget it and the story was told many times in later years when we returned to Manchester after the war.

Roy Sharples, 2013

Cokey Nolan

Cokey Nolan sells fish, three ha'pence a dish
Don't buy it, don't buy it, It stinks when you fry it.

Edward Nolan was really his name
Cokey was his claim to fame
He just tried to make a bob
He couldn't get a proper job

Salford kids did treat him wrong
On sight they sang his personal song
He'd turn to chase, then soldier on
The kids did scream, and they were gone
What more could poor old Cokey do
No chances of a job like me or you
Was it because of his IQ,
or what his teachers failed to do?

His dad - don't know, perhaps he'd gone
Maybe died or away had run
I know he lived with his old mam
He pushed a cart made from a pram
He loaded it with coal or coke
A better job he had no hope

In those past days in Salford City
When boys were tough and girls were pretty
Every one must pull their weight
But Cokey's job we all would hate
His clothes were dirty, his skin was caked
He really was in quite a state

Yes, I pulled coal in my old pram
To make a few bob as best I can
But Cokey did it as a job
It was his living was that few bob
I guess he tried to help his mam
By pulling a cart made from a pram

I don't think back then they had the dole
So what happened to old Cokey's role
The coalman came, and had a truck
What did that do to Cokey's luck
The coalman's truck could pull ten-ton
One hundredweight and Cokey's done
That's all that would fit on his cart
To move it took a lot of heart

So Cokey would drag his cart along
With heavy heart, no need for song
His head was bowed his back was bent
He went those places where he was sent

Down Derby Street, and Regent Road
Cokey pulled his heavy load
On top of that the kids would tease
Perhaps Claremont Street will bring some ease
For Cokey the man we kids did tease
We were not aware of Cokey's needs
Did he just need a little respect
Not the ridicule that he did get

He just kept pulling that nutty slack

Coal-yard to homes, forward and back
Cokey what was life really like for you
I guess it was just all you knew
A rotten way to gain your fame
But thousands do know of your name

I hope that Cokey before the end
You enjoyed your life and had some friends
So Cokey I raise my hat to you
You typify a spirit so true
You did not sit and mope around
You had your cart, and your coal round
You made a quid as best you could
You did your bit as a Salford lad would
So Cokey what more can I say
I'm sorry that I behaved that way

Ken Phoenix

Early Family History

My grandfather William Clark Luby Bracken was born 1867 (approx.) in O'Connell Street, Dublin where his father was a printer and believed to have connections to Sinn Fein. My mother said they left Ireland in a hurry when my grandfather was 3 years old and came to live in Robert Hall Street, Salford.

He was one of a family of 11 brothers and sisters. One brother - Thomas - emigrated to New Zealand and is famous for writing their national anthem as well as many poems and articles. On the 1881 census my grandfather was still living at home with his parents and siblings. He was 14 years old and his occupation listed as a printer compositor, the same as his father. The address was Eldon Street, Ordsall, which was almost opposite where I live now on Tatton Street. Coincidence, or what?

He married 'Aunt' Rose but never had any children. Work was difficult to find and he virtually lived as a tramp or 'journeyman', sleeping rough throughout the country searching for work. Story has it that one day when he returned home he found the house empty - all the furniture had been sold or pawned. My sister seems to think she even put the house up for sale. Sadly 'Aunt' Rose passed away and is buried in Weaste Cemetery. The grave papers are still in our possession stating the plot is for perpetuity.

He later met my grandmother Caroline Hall who was a widow with two children. She was a nurse and her family came from Barrow where her family were 'makers of clothes for the gentry' - her husband had been a (dental?) surgeon. They had two children Billy and Margery Baynes. (Looking on the family tree one daughter died the same year she was born).

My grandfather then married and had two children to Caroline. My mother was called Marcella Lucretia (Marie for short) born 1916 and Mona born 1918. My mother always told me her name came out of a book my grandfather was reading at the time. She always kept her name secret. (It was only recently we found when researching our family tree, that my grandfather had an older sister called Marcella born in 1865.)

The family lived in Renshaw Street, Patricroft (the street is still there but not the house). They were very poor and as grandfather was the only man in the street working, my grandmother ran a soup kitchen for poor people and the mill girls. She used to 'paint' the throats of the mill girls who suffered with the effects of working in the cotton trade. She also tended many neighbours who had TB who couldn't afford to pay for a doctor. The National Health Service did not exist.

During this time my grandfather's nephew, Billy Bracken, was orphaned and he was taken in and brought up with the other children. He was cousin to Marie and Mona.

When the First World War broke out, grandfather would be about 54 years old and because lots of men had joined the forces he was persecuted and very upset when a white feather was put through his door - inferring he was a coward. As he was a printer, a designated trade, he wouldn't have been allowed to go to war even if he had been a lot younger.

Grandfather was a member of the Labour Party and very important people used to visit him in Renshaw Street – I think one was called Kier Hardy and others were Members of Parliament. Grandmother was a founder member of the Ladies' section of the Labour Party. Politics were very much in the forefront when my mother was a young child. My mother used to listen in to the debates going on in the house from the top of the stairs. My grandfather was very strict and children were brought up in the Victorian tradition. Children should be seen and not heard! Apparently he believed that every mouthful of food should be chewed 32 times, one chew for every tooth in your head. There was never much food on the table in any case.

In 1926 during the General Strike, my mother, then about 10 years old, joined the march to Manchester, and Morris danced all the way to Manchester supporting the protesters. Don't know if her sister my Aunt Mona did the same as she was a couple of years younger but presumably all the family would have marched in support of the strikers.

In approximately 1927 when my mother was 11 years old her mother (Caroline) contracted TB and died. She had probably caught it from looking after all the poor people. Her first daughter Margery also caught it and was put in a sanatorium. Mother always called it Nab Top (don't know if it was the real name). She had her lung removed, recovered and lived into her eighties. She also trained as a nurse and worked hard all her life.

My Aunt Mona was known as a 'blue baby' and not sure if she didn't have her blood changed when she was born. My mother said that when they went to the baths, Mona used to come out of the changing rooms the attendant would never let her go into the water as with her condition she must have looked as if she had already been in the water too long!!

My mother was a fantastic swimmer and swam for Eccles and Patricroft in the swimming competitions. She won a Life-saving medal and a free pass to the baths. She also passed for grammar school but because she was the oldest and her father couldn't afford a uniform she had to go out to work. Mona, her sister, also passed for grammar school a couple of years later, but with wage earners being in the family the uniform could be afforded. You couldn't take your place without a uniform.

They were still a very poor family and times were very hard. My mother told of squeezing her feet into shoes which were too small and in later life this had its consequences. Her first job was in a furniture shop polishing 'miles' of furniture and she was given an apple and a penny a day for her lunch. Her wages had to be given to her father as part of the family income.

At some point she went to work at Greengate and Irwell Rubber Company where she met my father Bill Williams. He worked in the packing department and she worked in the finishing room. The company made all the waterproof coats for the police and had a contract with the military. She learned the 'rag trade' and ended up in charge of the girls working on finishing the coats, i.e. buttons etc. and also supervising the cutting out.

My parents courted for 8 years, during this time she had left home and gone to lodge with her future mother-in-law, my father's mother. Story goes that her father threw her out (don't know if this was right) and my grandmother took her in. Both my parents worked shift work and she said she only saw my father when she came home from work and he was going to work.

At the time my father's sister was still living at home her name was Marjorie. Sadly in 1936 at age 25 years she was killed in a road accident. She was on a cycling holiday in the Midlands and was knocked off her bike. My mother told me that she suffered from epilepsy which in those days was a big stigma so it wasn't spoken about. This was such a great loss to my grandma who had been widowed during the First World War and brought both children up on her own.

At the time she was widowed she was living in South Wales near to her in-laws. She had worked as a laundress before she married so had to look for work, as there were no benefits in those days. She did receive a small war widow's pension but it wasn't enough to bring up two young children. She saw an advert for a housekeeper in the Manchester area for a widower who had two children. She was successful and moved with her children to take up the position.

When the children were all grown up and working she borrowed £5 from her employer and put a deposit on a house on an estate round the corner. The house was semi-detached and cost £395. She managed to get a mortgage with, I presume, her ex-employer standing guarantor. She carried on working as a school cleaner and as a bar maid in the evenings. She had come a long way after being widowed in 1917. Shortly after buying the house she lost her daughter.

When war broke out in September 1939, my father was indentured to an estate agent and was no longer working at Greengate and Irwell Rubber Co. but my mother was still there. My father applied to join the army or the RAF and my mother applied for the WAFFS. Father's army papers came through first. They decided to get a special marriage licence and were married 3 weeks after war broke out before they went for training.

My mother said that when they were taking their vows and my mother's name 'Marcella Lucretia' was read out everyone gasped as nobody present, apart from my father, knew her full name. She always used the name Marie and only in the last few years of her life in her late seventies did she answer to her real name.

My grandfather had been living with his daughter my Aunt Mona and her husband in Audenshaw. There was a family row and he turned up at my gran's with nowhere to live. It was arranged that he could lodge with my paternal grandmother as a temporary measure. When my parents left to do their war service my grandfather was still there.

When I was born in 1942 my mother and I lived at my grans for two years until my mum found a house to rent around the corner on the same estate. My Dad was still in the army completing the full 6years. He came home on Compassionate Leave for the birth of my brother in October 1945 just after the war had ended. He was then demobbed and had to get used to civilian life - there were no combat stress organisations in those days to help people adjust.

I remember my grandfather coming round to our house and she used to dress his bad leg. He walked with a bone handled walking stick. I remember the last birthday card I got from him was when I was 5 years old. He was taken ill in early 1948 and passed away in March that year aged 81 years. He is buried in Southern Cemetery. Later that year my mother gave birth to my sister.

My grandfather's sister, Great Aunt Charlotte, lived in a bungalow in Moor Lane, Kersal. She had three children and one of them, either Bernard or Percy, disappeared and was never found. One son lived with his widowed mother and he was quite creepy. My mother would not let me be on my own with him - he used to wear a silk smoking jacket which was unusual to me.

Great Aunt Charlotte died in 1958. She was quite well off, her husband left her lots of shares in big companies. Her home was full of cut glass and 'posh' things. I was always afraid I might break something and was never very comfortable there, especially with the warnings about being on my own with her son, I would be about 16 yrs. old when she died. I don't think there was any contact after her passing.

This concludes the story of my family's early social history and their roots in Salford, dating back to the Victorian era.

Sylvia Sharples

Barmy Mick

It was on Cross Lane market Mick did his thing
When he'd set his truck up, out loud it did ring
Cos Mick was a showman and trader at that
He sold anything at the drop of a hat
When Mick clapped his hands, a signal so loud
That meant it was sold to someone in the crowd

'Now look at this ladies', he would shout out loud
Then show off his wares to the gathering crowd
'Here's ten pounds of value, but I don't want that'
Then came my favourite part of his act

'Not ten pounds, not eight pounds, would you give me seven?
If I sell it for that I will end up in heaven
Now listen you ladies to what I will do
Not 10, 9, 8, 7, it's five just for you'

Then up went the hands throughout the crowd
'Lady left', 'At the back', Mick shouted out loud
'Well, all of you ladies will a bankrupt make me
What's in the truck, now just let me see
Blankets, wool blankets, I have one or two
Let's see what I can do, just to please you'

'Not ten pounds, not eight pounds, would you give
me seven?
If I sell it for that I will end up in heaven
OK then ladies just take them away,
Six pounds a piece, is the best I can say
Too much for you dear, did I hear you say?
What happened on Friday, did you miss your pay day?
Hang on. God, I'm on my way
OK then, five pounds, but just for today'

Yes Mick did seem barmy to some of the crowd
Standing there clapping, and shouting out loud
He was quite clever, and good fun to see
Where are you now Mick, moved on just like me?

Ken Phoenix

Background to the crane poem

By the entrance to Salford Quays, which was Salford Docks, have stood for the last 40 odd years two very tall blue cranes. They are presently in a state of disrepair and Salford City Council are demolishing them as they say they are dangerous and make servicing the tram difficult. They were erected towards the end of the docks' life as state of the art modern cranes by the Manchester Ship Canal company.

Containerisation then emerged and the Manchester Docks, as they were then called, became redundant as did the jobs of dockers. After years of neglect the dock area was left neglected but then Salford Quays was built and developed as a tourist destination and the blue cranes were left in place at the dock entrance. Close to the cranes was a Tourist Information Centre and a small stainless steel, engraved sculpture called 'Four Corners', representing the four corners of the world. The engravings are artistic representations of the stories that some of the ex-dockers got together and there are poems and representations of what the docks meant to those dockers.

I got involved with a campaign to make this sculpture more visible in 2002 after I had been in a local group at O.C.A. performing a self penned musical entertainment on Salford Quays when the athletes arrived for the Commonwealth Games. A member of the group was Brian Nolan who had been one of the dockers' group involved in the making of the Four Corners. He was very disappointed that this sculpture had become almost invisible to the general public and that the vast majority of visitors did not see this artistic representation of the real dockers' lives, spirit and companionship. I attended several meetings with Brian, the sculptor Noah Rose, and council officials but nothing happened, and any move was considered too expensive.

Brian Nolan had obtained an 'A' level in English after retirement and wrote many stories, some of which we aired on the early community radio stations in Salford. He died a few years ago and the sculpture remains even more hidden as the trees around have grown and Tourist Information has moved into the Lowry. However it was featured recently at the relaunch of the Irwell Valley sculpture trail on the front page of the brochure, thanks to Andrea Bushell, (council worker), after I told her this story. As a result of this connection I have felt driven to pursue Brian's dying wish to increase the visibility of this sculpture. The poems are a result of this.

Jane Wood, September 2013

Four Corners

Part of the Irwell valley Sculpture Trail at Salford Quays

Thanks to the blue cranes
Symbols of the affluent Manchester Ship Canal Company.

Thanks to the Manchester Ship Canal Company
For providing employment for the hungry dockers

Thanks to the hungry dockers for sharing their stories
and spirit
On the low silver structure near the high rotting cranes
on the Quays.

Jane Wood

My Old Raincoat

My old gaberdine raincoat was special to me
It has those deep pockets, the reason you'll see
Then on the inside there was even more
Once full of goodies it dragged on the floor

You see my old man worked on the docks
The tricks they got up to would give you a shock
If cold in the winter, a carton would fall
The whisky would run, enough for them all
These men were masters, and would only break
One corner bottle, enough for their mates
The mugs would come out, a good measure inside
They'd drink it down, no bottles to hide

So what's this to do with my raincoat and me
You just read on, a secret you'll see
I must have looked daft on a hot summer's day
As Kenny and his raincoat did rush on their way

It was quite often my dad said to me
"You bring your raincoat to the hut on the quay"
So I would obey like a good docker's child
Me and my raincoat would cover some miles

Once I had found dad unloading a ship
A nod and a wink, and away we would slip
Into the hut, with a locked box inside
"You look at this", dad said with some pride

Then out came the bottles of whisky and such
All of these spirits my dad didn't touch
Then into my old mac's big pockets we'd hide
All of this booty he grabbed on the side

Then came the worst bit that I had to do
Fair play dad, it's all right for you
If I get caught, I'll probably get life
Just for a quick quid for you and your wife

Do I go through the fence, or out through the gate
I hope you are certain the copper's your mate
So off I do stroll with my heavy load
I walk pass the gate, and the copper as told
"Hey there, young Danny," I hear the man cry
My heart in my mouth, I know I will die
I hear my heart beating, and the bottles go chink
I know that's the end, I'm off to the clink
"Now you take your time, and go straight off home"
"It's not good for young lads to be walking alone"
As I raise my eyes, and look into his face
The copper gives a big wink, and I pick up my pace
Gosh that was a close one, I thought I was dead
The copper's my dad's mate. I know him as Fred

I reckon that Oliver Twist has nothing on me
I don't lift Hankies; I'm big time you see
I've been wrapped in suit cloth, which sometimes got wet
No, not from the rain but from this poor child sweat
When you're twelve years old, pilfering's no fun
But if your dad's on the docks, it just has to be done

Now those who knew my dad, would often say
That Danny's an angel, butter melt - no way
Now his young lad Kenny, he's a fine lad
He'll grow up an angel just like his dad

Ken Phoenix

The Pitman's Daughter (song)

In Salford town, on a sunny day
You were walking slowly by
The sunshine lighting up your smile,
beneath the pale blue sky.
I picked some daisies, made a chain
and I offered them to you
By the Ship Canal, near the Mode Wheel Lock
You turned my world pale blue

We walked a while and I hid a smile
when you told me where you were from
You described the Irwell Valley, love
with sweet poetry and aplomb.
And I knew that you were dreaming
though your thoughts and motives fine
For I worked with your own dear father down
the cold, dark Agecroft mine

In Salford town, on a sunny day
You were walking slowly by
The sunshine lighting up your smile,
beneath the pale blue sky.
I picked some daisies, made a chain
and I offered them to you
By the Ship Canal, near the Mode Wheel Lock
You turned my world pale blue

Albert Thompson
(using words supplied by members of the Ordsall
Creative Writing Group)

It Just Goes On

The old man looked at me from across the street,
"Hello, lad" he uttered with a low guttural tone
I didn't know him but I knew what he meant,
His greeting wasn't words but an acknowledgement
A fellow Salfordian just getting through life
The old lady nodded as she passed by,
The rain fell across her face like tears
Her once proud body bent and hunched with age,
Her bags seemed heavy but she refused my help
In Salford, even if it's offered, help is never taken
The children kicked their ball down the cobbled street
Dreams of Old Trafford and Wembley never to be granted
Their knees are dirty, their shoes are scuffed,
But their hearts are still pure
Not yet tarnished by the pressure of age
The dull roofs shining with the sky's tears,
While grimy streets throb with the sound of traffic
Salford life doesn't slow down,
It just goes on.

Chris Thorn

Cross Lane Pubs

From the end of Barbary Coast we'll trip,
For a quick one into the SHIP
Past Palace, Opera House and before cockle-shop,
into the WELLINGTON for another we hop.
Waltz past the station, skip over Lane Hodge,
A sly-one into the FALCON dodge,
March past the barracks with big drum beat,
Old friends in the BUCK we'll surely meet.
Across Liver we'll do the Palais Glide,
And into the MARKET HOTEL we slide
Now watch it with those quick, quick, slows,
Behind our belts it's Red Rose,
Meditation halts with old world charms,
Try a twist into the BUTCHER'S ARMS.
A turn for the better Boddington's beer,
Back to the drum beat FUSILIER,
Hands, knees and bumpsy dip,
Into the GRAPES next to the Salford Hipp.
Waltzing again to favourite mediation,
Reverse turn into the CORPORATION.
Fandango into the CRAVEN HEIFER if you are able
And quickly down Threlfalls Blue Label.
No dancing here, it's just on the drinking list
ROYAL OAK (mad-house) sadly missed.
Now once again with your quick. quick, slows -
Take your partners to the TAVERN and go.
You'll never make it, and that's my bet,
Five more places to dance to yet. '
Stagger slightly into the WILTON for pint of best.

And unsteady you are in the LONDON NOR' WEST
Come, come lads, backs to the wall.
STATION hour, and it's Whitley/Greenall.
My thoughts of dancing at now far away,
As we stagger into the old RAILWAY.
Into the finishing post with a final lurch,
Sam Smiths Tadcasters - our last one
-THE CHURCH

Stan Kelly (1975)
as quoted in the book 'Cross Lane' by Tony Flynn

Coming Home (song)

We're coming home, back to where we belong
Coming home been away for too long

Climbed up mountains, sailed the seven seas
Felt the heat of the desert, seen the arctic freeze
We've travelled the world, over land and sea
Ridden the waves, on the ocean free

Flown through clouds, way up high
Seen a rainbow arched across the sky
Coming home, back to where we belong
Coming home been away for too long

Tired of roaming want to settle down
Laze in the sun,till the day is done
Want to hear the sound, of a nightingale's song
Coming home, been away for too long

We will never forget, the sights we have seen
The people we met, the places we have been
Now we are coming home back to where we belong
Coming home, been away for too long

Song by Madge Bown (words and tune)
and Mike Scantlebury (tune)

My Name

Who can give me my name?
A parent, A guardian, A priest, A tribe

Who can steal my name?
The slave master or the identity thief.

Christians are Christened,
The Sioux have name giving ceremonies,

But the Christians civilised the Sioux and gave
them Christian Names.

Who can change my name?
A husband, A Liverpudlian, My friends, conquerors

Who can change a city's name?
The dictator, the empire builder, the developer or

The Boundary Commission?
Salford identity thieves.

Competition for the name of the proposed new ward,
e.g. Salchester
Manford
Medialand!!!!!

Jane Wood

Demolition

Right or Wrong?

Ordsall is a small triangle in the southern tip of the City of Salford. Surrounded on all sides by major roads its streets were narrow, with mainly two up and two down houses with no hot water or inside toilets. The people were friendly and family orientated, many of the children living in the same street as their parents. The old families of Ordsall came to Salford in the late 1800s to work on the building of the Ship Canal. Some stayed on to make it their home and bring up their young children. Many of the people worked locally, the men on the docks, or in local factories, the women in the mill, on shifts 6 till 2 or 2 till 10, or in the clothing industry as machinists. In the early days people met and married within the estate, thus building up a web of relations.

As well as working in the area the people did their shopping on Regent Road, where you could buy whatever you needed, from a packet of needles to a gas boiler or bedroom suite. A Councillor once asked me why the people of Ordsall don't look outwards; I told her that we had no need to, as we had everything we needed within our reach. This made us very territorial; a man was once asked by a newcomer why he walked from Weaste three times a week for a drink. His simple answer, 'I was born here'. A lady called one day; she was doing a survey, and after a couple of questions she said , 'You may think this a funny question but can you tell me where you live?'

I said, 'Ordsall in Salford'. She smiled and said. 'Everyone here knows exactly where they are' - unlike Trinity, where she found the majority thought they lived in Manchester!

In the seventies the City Council started to pull Ordsall down, starting at the Lane and moving across the estate to Trafford Road. We were given a house with a garden or a maisonette, a lot of them built of concrete. People were moved from one side of the estate to the other or from the top to the bottom. During the upheaval many people lost their homes and were moved to other areas of the City; not all of them wanted to go but they had no choice, as there were not enough houses left for everyone. In the early nineties the powers that be decided that the estate needed refurbishing and the concrete houses were to be given a skin of brick and a driveway. This meant that some people would lose their homes again.

We are now in 2010, and they are building again, but this time nobody is to lose their home. Instead we are bringing people into the estate to share what has been built up over the years. So was it necessary? To tear families apart to build a new Ordsall? Some people will say it was for the better, but others say that the houses could have been modernized and some of the old buildings saved. They were happy the way they were, in their own little street with family and friends; some now feel isolated in their little flats. Will the new houses being built today stand the test of time for a hundred years? Will the family once again form the base of the new Ordsall estate? Only time will tell.

Madge Bown

Lighting The Legend - the legend (song)

Chorus:
1, 2, 3, 4, 5, make Ordsall legends come alive.
6, 7, 8, 9, 10, from Ordsall Hall down to Woden's Den.
From 10 to 20, so it goes, every year the story grows.
The fireworks flash and the lantern glows.
The Legend's a legend Ordsall knows.

The Spirit of Ordsall we know the most,
is the White Lady walking like a ghost.
She floats in clouds and holds her lamp,
till she finds the empty Lads' Ghost Camp.

In the Sea of Dreams the current swirls,
as we pan for gold and dive for pearls.
We look for bones far from the sea,
when we dig for archaeology.

Chorus

The Green Banana's not the only fruit.
I like it here, it seems to suit.
I think I'll stay if you'll let me, mate.
I'll give you a hand to unload that crate.

I'll work on the Docks and not let you down,
if you let me call this 'Salford Town'.
The song is wrong, you must agree.
Salford's a City since 1270.

Chorus

For 20 years we've seen cold and rain,
700 years and back again.
Our hearts are bright, our souls to cheer,
with a thousand lights and more this year.

We've cycled, re-cycled and mixed and brewed,
the chemicals of work and food.
The Vikings came from days of yore,
but the dinosaurs were here before.

Chorus

Mike Scantlebury (words and new tune,
based on a traditional song)

Haze

Snowflakes fall
Cold winds blow
A hazy sun shines on ice and snow
The branches of the shrubs and trees
Shiver in the winter breeze
The berries all by now have gone
What will all the birds feed on?
Will they last until the spring
When again we will hear them sing?
The robin with his breast of red
The blackbird high upon a tree
A thrush with speckles on his chest
Will he be looking for a brand new nest?
We can only hope and pray
That we see them all another day

Madge Bown, 2011

Headed

It starts as any other day. You drive to see
your new in-laws. You are tired. But your wife is insistent.
You reach the Black Country. And die: that
is why it is called black, drive
to Birmingham and don't come back.

You wake in the worst B Movie you have ever seen.
There is no intermission. Then you learn the awful
truth. This is your new existence as a crippled man.

Your old loves are like fingers of ice on the winter
window pane. They distort and vanish with the suns
warmth. Your best friend sits with you, and pushes your
drip as you walk again: she was your wife: your final love.

The years of pain and therapies to bring you back
to life. Your wife leaves for an un-crippled
woman. Now you sing on stage, you have soul,
because pain is an
old friend of yours.

Jonathan Thomason

This Land is your Land (song)

LOCAL CHORUS: This land is your land,
this land is my land
From Sainsbury's car park to the Stowell Spire island
From the Red Rose Forest to Media City
This land was made for you and me

As I went walking, that ribbon of highway
I saw above me that endless skyway
I saw below me that Irwell Valley
This land was made for you and me

Chorus

I roamed and I rambled and followed my footsteps
Past the sparkling towers of her diamond buildings
And all around me a voice was sounding
This land was made for you and me

Chorus

When the sun came shining, Well I was strolling
With the people waving as the rain was going
The crowds were chanting as the clouds were parting
This land was made for you and me

CHORUS

New words by Jane Wood
(to an old tune by Woody Guthrie)

ORIGINAL CHORUS: This land is your land,
this land is my land
From California to the New York Island
From the redwood forest to the Gulf Stream waters
This land is made for you and me

Woody Guthrie

Technology

It's hard to think of times past
When the world was not so vast
News took weeks to filter down
To every village and every town.

Today, world events are broadcast
In a flash on TV's, radios and podcast.
No time to digest the facts
And decide how we should react.

Everyone is in the public eye
CCTV makes it hard to deny
Where we are throughout the day
Whether we are at work or play.

Big Brother is watching you -
We never thought that would come true!
Too late now for protestations
We have to live with our indignations.

We did not read our crystal ball
Warnings were written on the wall.
Feeble voices whispered their dismay
But technology is here to stay.

Sylvia Sharples, November 2010

St Ignatius church (song): Jane Wood

Ignatius, well he was a soldier
He fought for what he thought was right
At 100 years old, his head was wet and cold
And he was in a terrible plight
His enemies watched while he crumbled
Where he lay they had plans of great dread
"What we need now are a-part-ee-ments
Let him rot, put a flat up instead."

Chorus:
Then along came his friends, his very good friends
We'll fight for your life, they said
Then along came his friends, his very good friends
and helped them to mend his head

So his friends they all wrote letters
They fought with a pen in their hand
They called on learned people
and then they formed a band
'Cos heritage, it is an earner
It's what we do well in this land
So Ignatius stopped its leak
To the world they did speak
And they all worked hand in hand

Chorus:
So along came his friends, his very good friends
We'll fight for your life, they cried
So along came his friends, his very good friends
Who looked at the building with pride.

Flowers of life

We enter this life in the hygienic hospital
Strewn with Carnations and White Roses.
The scent of new life and hope for a better
happier world of fragrance.

Our new home is full with the blossoms
of aromatic plants. To drown out the pungent
aromas of babies and nappies. The stench
of the blessings of the stock to the young
loving couple. You are so blessed
with the beauty of nature.

As we go to school girls, learn of love and life.
Boys learn of war and death. But remember
to fetch some dog pee Daiseys for mother
walking through the park. She adds them
to the tulips of the guild of her husband,
such a good provider!

Then it is on to the love roses: the signal
of the hot physical, fragrant physical
world of our lover. Truly holistic.
The magic of touches the
wizardry of lone poetry.
The heady intoxication of our
all our too rampant hormones.

Life starts over.
For us it is senility and tending our back garden.
Full of colour. The Freesias, heady
scent of the Climbing Ivy. Bombarding our senses
with the import that modern life lacks:
no taste or fragrance to anything now!
Our senses are not dimmed,
it is modernity which lacks vim.
Now we wait only for
the Lillies of Death

Jonathan Thomason

Moonlight

Above the earth
as the sun goes down
a light begins to shine.
It's from another planet
but of a different kind.
A planet with no people ,
animals or birds
where no grass grows
no river flows
or flowers bloom in spring
with its treeless mountains
and valleys
with no running streams.
Its priceless gift to Mother Earth
are beautiful moonbeams.

Madge Bown,
1998

Bed Torture

I loved my grandmother to bits,
but she was so Scottish.
And they make children tougher there. Not
inclined to moan when their skin is removed
by instrument of medieval torture.

I was staying there, and the snow was out. I got
her to shut the windows after only 2 hours
whining. 'Is there no away to warm the beds?'
'We could invite the sea serpent in
to preheat it for a few hours' she
suggested. 'No really' I pleaded.

'And there was me forgetting you're a
soft Southerner. We can deploy the bed
warmer' she suggested. 'A hot water
bottle?' I asked in excitement.
'Ah, you could call it that' she replied, wheeling in
this medieval torture implement from beneath
where she still had the last four year's tax returns,
in case she had a bad virus and got bored.

It was metal. It was not rubber. You fill it with
lava from the permanently erupting volcano
conveniently located by the whisky still:
fire water indeed.

It worked just like a hot water bottle. But if
your foot touched the glowing metal
it removed the skin from your foot.
And it was off to A&E.
Where, luckily, they have central heating,
for the soft, injured, Southerners

Jonathan Thomason

Nature's Revenge

Oil and gas and nuclear power
Are we living in an ivory tower?
Nature seems to show who’s boss
Then we begin to count the cost.

It’s time for us to now take stock
Or all our heads will be on the block
All of nature lives in peace
Man alone takes the golden fleece.

We should consider what is right
It’s time now to see the light.
We should not pander to our greed
Only take that which we need.

Poverty and need is all around
Crops are dying in barren ground.
Climate change is moving fast
For many peoples the dye is cast.

Resolutions should be made
For new foundations to be laid.
To consider each and every nation
And help them out of deprivation.

Sylvia Sharples
March 2011

Rich man, poor man

Some people may be rich and some poor but what does it really mean? Does it mean that you are wealthy and have plenty of money? Could it be that if you are rich you are happy and have everything you want, and if you are poor you are sad and have no future?

What would happen if the rich man suddenly became poor - if due to some misfortune he lost all his wealth, would his friends wave to him from their expensive cars when they pass him as he walks down the street? Would he still be asked to dine at the high class restaurants although he could not afford to pay? His life would be changed forever, but then maybe not; if he worked hard it could be that he can climb up the ladder again. But then would he really want to join the hustle and bustle again after making new friends at the bottom of the ladder where he is accepted for himself and not for how much money he may have, how large his house is, or what size car he drives. And would he want to give up his new found freedom?

Now a poor man can become a rich man by winning or being left a large amount of money. He could buy a large house, a new car and have rich new friends. But being at the top would he miss his old friends at the bottom who cannot afford to join him on his high priced holidays - abroad unless he paid the bill! And would he be at home in his new surroundings, with people he has no connection with?

Maybe he will enjoy the life of leisure, being able to buy whatever he wants without worrying about the cost. But even a rich man can be very poor, for example in health. Some rich people have money but live a simple life with friends they have known since childhood. Many poor people live their lives to the full, doing things that do not cost a great deal of money but brings them a lot of enjoyment.

So you see riches are not only about money. You can be rich in other ways: having a loving family, good health and true friends makes you a rich person.

Rich man or poor man, your life is what you make it, with or without money.

Madge Bown, 2013

The Pyramid is crumbling

The pyramid is crumbling and tumbling
Falling down, so that no one is higher than the other
We look around and see each other on the same level.
No one is better than another. Everyone is valuable
on the ground
Nothing to prop up, energies profound

The pyramid of slavery
Kept the dead inside alive in the dark and
Called them mummy.
Kept the slaves struggling and scrambling up the
tilted walls
Without time to wonder why they did it for their masters
Just to stay alive for the dynasties to sit upon them
Until they died and called them mummy

The cranes are crumbling
Falling down, so no one is higher than the other
We look around and see each other on the same level
We see the spirit, the fun, the love and caring we all
can share
Everything to live for, energy flows around

The cranes of near slavery
Keeping the workers in queues to avoid starvation
Called them bosses
Kept the dockers stuggling, covered in asbestos for
pennies more

No time to wonder why they did it for their masters
Just to feed their growing families to die in wars
Until the Manchester Ship Canal company died
and became Peel Holdings

Jane Wood

Our World

Flying high above the earth
Looking down from above,
we can see the valleys
and the mountains high.
Fast flowing rivers
wind down to the sea
and fields of green grasses
are blowing in the wind
But then we see the chimneys
blowing out their smoke.
All the pollution rising from below.
Ice that once was pearly white
is now a dusky grey.
Forests spread around our world
are being cut away.
We don't have time to ponder
We don't have time to wait.
All of us must do our bit,
before it is too late.

Madge Bown, 2004

Rivers of Life

In our history man has gravitated
To the rapidly flowing Rivers of life.
Streams, rivers, the sea and Lakes
Always fascinated by the wild waters
The fish, loads of mammals and plants
An exercise in ecology laid before us
The motorways of transfer of goods
The Rivers of our historic transactions
Fascinated by its tumbling, foaming
And life giving nature. They are life

Go down to the riverside village
And do Merchant trade with me
Food, clothes, engines and our stories
Of how the water brings life to us all
Bring your fish, and your rod and line
And we will catch our evening meal!
I will baptise you into new life afresh
And you can bury your old who died
To celebrate the flows of human lives
And you can marry my young daughter
But do not tumble into the dark water
Or is surely as the water gives life
It'll take yours away from your body.
And lie as quietly as murderers do!

Jonathan Thomason

TV Extra

The Oasis is Salford college doing media
and performance: the BBC is 3 miles down
the road. Desiring students trained in
the performing arts. Next door is the
Lowry, devouring talent and delighting
in individuals strutting their stuff
in a creative way.
Yes I have strutted, and sung and entertained
Manchester. Like a trained monkey dancing
on a hotplate in the hope of their evening
meal. The staff at the Lowry now recognise
me as a singer. I should be dead. This is the
best life ever.
A life I did not dare to hope lay hidden in
my damaged brain: my car accident surgically
removed 30% of it. But left behind the grey matter
that runs its fingers on the sheet music
and compels my voice to oscillate in a rhythmic
Fashion
During the week we can see Oasis Academy irrigating the
dry lands between Eccles and the Quays. Dispensing
our nuggets of media gold, to amuse and train the
students of future. They are our future. We must
train them well. 'I am you father!' said Darth
To his son and future - the Luke!
I have time, I have talent I need to engage
with 6th form psyche: to winnow out the
grains that will delight future televisions: when

the Quays becomes Media City UK. When I will sit
with joy and watch the students I helped spring
into flower.
Blooming performance brilliance! That
will entertain the world. Singing, act-
ing and stroking the brains of the hard-
working for a while. Designed light
and joy into the lives of everybody
who sees and hears their collective brilliance
And yes, I am not bad either. When
I'm not working as a TV extra, I will be
working to make the students create TV extra!

Jonathan Thomason

Taking a break

Took a short break im my comfort zone,
Felt good, my blood pressure went down
So I decided to stay

For Andrea

Leaves practise death as a beautiful display
Human cells more often hide it away

Clifton Country Park: The Irwell Valley Sculpture Trail

The dog barked madly at the iron man
He sniffed at the iron woman
And wagged his tail at the wooden horse

Jane Wood

Hope Casualty

Sitting in the room of gloom
Waiting for the call
It's half past five in Casualty
And mum has had a fall.

It's seven o'clock, not many left
Our turn is soon I hope
No matter how few patients
The staff don't seem to cope

At eight o'clock, I'm getting dry
I go to get a Coke
We club together all our change
Then the drinks machine is broke

My sister's on her mobile
And I've just finished off my book
It's half past nine, the boredom hits
My mum gives a nasty look

We watch the patients come and go
Our envy turns to hate
It's half past ten and we're still here
No one's had our wait

We finally see a doctor
We finally get the nod
He sends her for an X ray
Another queue, "Good God"

It's half past twelve, we're back again
The staff have all gone home
A new shift is just starting
We're feeling all alone

My mum seems so much better now
They think there's nothing wrong
So off we go, although relieved
Why did it take so long?

Chris Thorn

Disappointment: -
Things could have been different

Tina stood before the mirror and ran her hands over her dress. Yes, I think that looks very nice, she thought as she took one last glance over her shoulder. “Are you nearly ready?” she heard her mother shout from the bottom of the stairs. “Yes, I will be down in a minute or two,” she replied as she picked up her handbag and gave her hair a final quick brush.

Tina's mother was waiting in the small hallway. “Here is your hat, dear. You do look nice in that dress, the colour suits you very well.” “Thank you, mother. I hope we both enjoy ourselves now that we are all dressed up.” “I am sure we will,” said her mother, picking up two parcels wrapped in fancy paper, and her rather large hand bag. Tina and her mother were going to her cousin Ruby's wedding, who was going to marry a man she had met while on holiday. Although she had told Tina what he was like and how they met, Tina had never actually seen him.

They walked into the church and sat down on the bride's side, alongside their relatives and friends. “This is a very nice church isn’t it? Your father and I were married here, nearly thirty years ago.” “Yes, I know mother, it is a beautiful place,” said Tina as she looked round the church.

The organ started to play as Ruby and her father began to walk down the aisle, and as they reached the front the groom turned his head.

Tina's heart missed a beat. It can't be, she whispered to herself as she recognized the man standing next to Ruby. "That's Harry." "Harry," repeated her mother. "You mean the man you met on holiday?" "Yes, mother. The man who wanted to marry me."

As the bride and groom passed by, Harry caught Tina's eye and gave her a smile and a wink. All she could do was nod her head in reply.

As the night progressed Tina went over to spend a few moments with Ruby who was standing all alone near the dance floor. "You look beautiful," she said giving her a kiss on the cheek. "Thank you, Tina. I hope that one day you will meet someone as nice and loving as my Harry." "Where is he?" asked Tina, glancing round the room. "He is dancing with an old friend of his. He will be back in a few minutes."

Tina had already noticed Harry in the far corner of the room chatting to a young woman. So she told Ruby that she was going to see if her mother was all right. "I will see you later, Ruby, bye." "Good-bye, Tina."

Everybody seemed to be enjoying themselves. Her Mother was dancing with an old family friend and Tina had found a seat near the bar. As she sat sipping her drink, Harry appeared from nowhere. He was drunk, as he usually was on the holiday. "How are you, Tina?" he asked as he pulled up a stool and sat down. "A long time, no see."

"Are you a friend of Ruby's?" "I'm her cousin," she replied abruptly. "Oh, I see. I saw you speaking to her. I hope you didn't tell her we had met before." "No, I did not," said Tina. "That's all right, then. There is no need to tell her, is there?"

"I will be seeing you quite often now that I am part of the family. It will be like old times," he said, putting his arm round her shoulder. "Are you disappointed we never kept in touch?" Tina laughed out loud.

"Disappointed?" she said removing his arm from her shoulder. "No, I am not, Harry. I think that I had a very lucky escape. Ruby is more than welcome to you," she said, raising her glass. "Cheers, and good-bye, Harry."

Madge Bown

A Day Trip to Ireland

It was a day in January in the late 60's and my then partner had purchased a converted trawler from a guy in White Rock, Northern Ireland.

We had waited days for a suitable forecast to go and collect the boat, there had been nothing but gales. Now the weather was set fair so we booked the midnight ferry, hurriedly collected our gear together. The gear consisted of pots, pans, sleeping bags, life jackets, flares and enough food to last at least 3 days. We looked like hillbillies with our noisy rucksacks jingling along.

A friend of ours called Johnny had a skipper's ticket and was a Manchester Ship Canal pilot and had offered to bring the boat over to a boatyard in Tarleton, where the boat was going to be refurbished.

We arrived in Belfast about 6am, gathered our belongings and went to get a taxi to White Rock. There were dozens of people queuing at the taxi ranks, armed soldiers were patrolling the docks, quite a culture shock. The whole area was very tense. Taxi drivers were walking up and down the lines of people asked where they were bound for. Lots were refused a taxi but we were lucky, White Rock seemed to be OK.

We bundled our gear into the cab and explained why we had such strange luggage.

We arrived at the house in White Rock, which belonged to the owner of the boat, who it turned out was a member of the judiciary. We were ushered into a small visitors' room. We had left our gear on the doorstep.

Suddenly, very quietly, a housekeeper appeared and her employer asked her to bring us tea and toast. She hardly spoke a word. A large tray was brought in with the tea and toast. We were really hungry.

We soon demolished all the toast and marmalade and sat back. Next another lot of toast and marmalade appeared as if by magic. Johnny and I had the same sense of humour - no words were spoken and I daren't look at him or I would have given way to hysterics, so we nodded and ate the second lot. We thought that was it, but no - yet another lot of toast appeared. This happened several times. It's a wonder we didn't choke ourselves.

Now it was down to business. The boat, The Golden Dawn, had been brought off her mooring in Strangford Lock and was alongside the small pier. We were given a tour of the boat, paperwork completed and everything checked for our impending voyage. The owner told us there was some peat for the pot-belly stove in the fo'o'sle. He had arranged for a pilot to take us through the loch where local knowledge was essential.

We reached the end of the loch and said farewell to our pilot. It was now up to us to cross the Irish Sea, heading for the River Ribble. It would take many hours.

It was freezing cold so we decided to light the fire - none of us had used peat before. It must have been too damp as the whole of the boat filled with acrid smoke. So the fire was out of the question. We had to heave to until we could see where we were going.

We took it in turns to steer, my partner and I under Johnny's directions as he needed to sleep before taking the night watch, when we would be passing the Isle of Man.

I found it difficult to sleep, so was awake for most of the voyage. The sea was flat calm. We were so lucky to be underway.

Around 10 o'clock that night I was in the wheelhouse keeping Johnny company, we were passing close to the Chicken Rock off the Isle of Man. We had managed to get some music on a small transistor radio, when suddenly blasting loud and clear came the theme from The Onedin Line, which was popular at that time. We couldn't stop laughing, it was a magical moment.

The rest of the voyage passed without mishap and at dawn we were approaching Morecambe Bay, when a thick sea mist set in. We heard ships passing some distance away. The entrance to the Ribble would be difficult to find under these conditions so the skipper said it was better to come to an anchor and hope the mist would clear during the morning.

We organised an anchor watch and two went below to grab an hour's sleep.

We were on a time schedule to make the boatyard at Tarleton at high water as that was the only time we could get through the lock, when the canal and river were the same height. We were quite concerned as it would mean spending another 24 hours at sea if we couldn't make the high water deadline.

A few hours later the mist had cleared so we upped anchor and set off for the River Ribble. We then had to find the smaller River Douglas which led to the canal at Tarleton. This river was difficult to navigate, just little sticks, marking the channel.

We just made it in time and the water had levelled in the lock and we sailed into Tarleton.

It was a memorable trip and I still laugh when I see marmalade and toast and hear The Onedin Line theme tune.

Happy days.

Sylvia Sharples
May 2010

Acknowledgements

This book has been put together by members of Ordsall Creative Writers, who meet every Wednesday morning from 10am to 12 noon at Ordsall Community Arts on Robert Hall Street, next to the Library.

They are part of Ordsall Trust, who can be found on Facebook and at:

http://www.OrdsallTrust.com/

This book forms part of the BBC's 'All Our Stories' project 2013, supported by Heritage Lottery Fund. Thanks to the funders for help with a new website and organising oral histories and interviews recorded over the years in East Salford, which have now been put up on on the internet and made available to the general public.

The link is http://www.OrdsallWords.wordpress.com/

Thanks to all the contributors, who retain copyright of their individual contributions.

www.ingramcontent.com/pod-product-compliance
Ingram Content Group UK Ltd.
Pitfield, Milton Keynes, MK11 3LW, UK
UKHW020237250726
13967UKWH00001B/417

9 781291 593433